Maryanne Resumes Her journey

Interrupted Bridal Journey

Part two

By:*Kent Hamillton*

© 2016

COPYRIGHT © 2016 BY: KENT HAMILTON

Printed in USA

© Copyright 2016

All Rights Reserved

No part of this publication may be reproduced or transmitted in any form whatsoever, electronic, or mechanical, including photocopying, recording, or by any informational storage or retrieval system without express written, dated and signed permission from the author.

By reading this you accept these terms and conditions.

TABLE OF CONTENTS:

Chapter 1 5
Chapter 2 11
Chapter 3 15
Chapter 4 19
Chapter 5 23
Chapter 6 27
Chapter 7 31
Chapter 8 37
Chapter 9 43
Chapter 10 47

Chapter 1

Maryanne ran her hand for the thousandth time over her stomach. The thought that there was a budding life inside it filled her with wonder. There was still no external evidence of her pregnancy, since she was only two months into her term, but she certainly felt different. Partly physically, and she had occasional morning sickness, but far more emotionally. She felt more in tune with God or The Universe, she wasn't sure which, and that she was fulfilling her destiny in some way. There is little that is more satisfying, and little that leads to a greater feeling of completeness, than the conviction that one is fulfilling one's life's work. Plus she felt it brought her and Peter closer together.

Peter, since he didn't have a new life growing inside of him, couldn't feel the same way as Maryanne. However, he was able to see that her pregnancy was making her blossom, and that made him happy. Their life together was idyllic. Although she missed him while he was away on his duties, the time they spent together when he was back in Omaha, made up for it amply.

At about two months into her pregnancy, a letter arrived postmarked Baltimore. Maryanne left it on the kitchen table for two days before opening it; she dreaded its contents, and the inevitable pall that she assumed it would cast over everything. She finally decided she could delay it no longer.

> Dear Child,
>
> Your letter both saddened and gladdened my heart. Talk about trying to confuse an old lady!
>
> I am sure that you expect me to tell you that you have made a mistake, and that you will regret this, and all

kinds of similar admonishments. And, yes, these may all be true. You have made a mistake, in the long term, and you may very well regret this. But I understand that, at this time, you are exceedingly happy, and that alone is enough to give me joy.

When we were discussing your marriage to Mr. Worthington, you made reference to my possibly having had male friends before meeting your uncle, and you may have inferred from my reaction that there was more to that subject than I had previously admitted. There is a lot from my younger days that I never told you. There's a lot that I never told your uncle, too! Maybe now is as good a time as any to unburden myself. I have carried the secret for too long.

I did meet a man before your uncle, and we were very much in love. I fell pregnant, and since we were not married, and there was no prospect of that happening, I had to go away for a time. The scandal of an unwed mother in our family would have broken it, if it had become generally known, and so they manufactured a reason for my leaving. I had the baby, and immediately gave it up for adoption. After a suitable interval I returned. The man I was in love with came with me initially, but as I got larger and larger from the pregnancy, his interest waned, and not long before I gave birth he disappeared. I have never seen him, or the child I gave birth to, since.

That is one of the main reasons that, when your parents died within a short time of each other, I was more than happy to take you in. You were the child that I could never have kept. By that time I was married to your uncle, and it seemed that we could not have any children, and we were reasonably financially secure, so it all worked out. And, if I may say so, raising you was one of the most rewarding things I have ever done!

I feel better for having shared that! It's been sitting heavily on my heart for many a year. The fling that I had, although unplanned, got the need for heady romance out of me, and made me content with your uncle. And contentment is more than one can expect out of life!

I hope you don't think any the worse of me after this revelation. I imagine not, since I was subject to the same desires and influences that you were. You at least have put the horse before the cart!

The only advice I can give you is to hold fast to the joy you are currently experiencing, and remember it well. Since there is every likelihood that times will get tougher. Things change, men's attentions change, what was a joy becomes a burden. I don't wish these changes on you; however I anticipate them from experience.

I hope that your joy remains for as long as it may.

Your loving,

Aunt Hilda.

Maryanne sat and looked out the window. She understood that things could change. However, the way she felt now, it seemed that her happiness could go on forever.

A few weeks later, a letter arrived from San Francisco. This was the one Maryanne had been dreading the most. This time, however, since she didn't waste time before reading it; she didn't want the prospect looming over her like a cloud, any longer than necessary.

Dear Maryanne,

I don't need to tell you that your actions have surprised me immensely. Throwing over a comfortable, secure prospect, for what can only be described as uncertainty and almost guaranteed penury, leaves me at a loss for explanation. However, the very limited interaction that I have had with the opposite sex has shown me that many of their actions are without logical cause.

You may care to picture the scene in your mind. My standing on the platform at San Francisco station, flowers in hand, awaiting with interest to see you alight. When instead, George and Martha Thackeray disembark, and come and break the news to me as gently as they are able. It put me in the role of the jilted suitor, one in which I had no experience, and for which I have no particular taste.

I don't mind telling you that, from the time of your acceptance letter, until the news was broken to me by the Thackerays, I built up an image in my mind of us happily married, with you ensconced in my house, and a few children added to the scene after a while. The bombshell delivered by the Thackerays effectively destroyed that image.

However, if you were to see sense now, I would be prepared to forgive, and allow us to return to our previous plan. I could arrange to have your marriage to this soldier annulled, and we could resume where we left off, effectively. I urge you to consider the future, and take me up on this offer.

Yours etc.

Thomas Worthington.

The letter depressed Maryanne rather. She had not wanted to hurt or disappoint Thomas, but it was obvious that she had. The image of his waiting expectantly at the station was rather pathetic, and she was grieved to have been the cause of it.

The possibility of taking up his offer did not cross her mind for a second as a pursuable option, but she wondered whether he would have made the offer had he known of her imminent confinement.

Luckily he had not mentioned the money. It would seem that the money was the least of his concerns. She was glad of that, since she still had no idea how she was going to repay him. Peter's salary was not large, and most of it seemed to be consumed by their living expenses.

She put the letter away and resolved not to answer it. She had made things plain in her most recent letter to Thomas, and there was no point in reiterating her feelings.

Chapter 2

About five months later, during a period when Peter was away on duty, Maryanne was sitting at home, crocheting some baby clothes, when there was a knock at the door. She opened it, to reveal a prosperous looking gentleman on the doorstep. He said nothing. She was about to ask what she could do for him, when she realized who it had to be.

"Hello, Thomas."

"Hello, Maryanne."

They stood looking at each other for a couple of seconds. Maryanne was loth to ask him into the house. She could see no purpose in his visit, other than to disrupt her life, but at the same time politeness dictated that she invite him in. They could not stand looking at each other on the doorstep.

"Won't you come in, please?"

"Er, that could be awkward if your husband is present."

"He is away on duty."

"All right then, if I may."

Maryanne led him into the parlor, and closed the door.

Thomas looked at the chair he was offered, a little longer than was required, before seating himself. He was not used to sitting on such old furniture.

Maryanne offered him a drink, but he declined.

He got straight to business. "Maryanne, since you did not answer my letter, I decided to come and talk to you, to try and bring you round."

Maryanne interrupted. "Thomas, I fear that you trip will have been in vain. I understand that the lifestyle as your wife would have been much more opulent than this" - she waved her hand to take in the house - "but it is the life I have chosen, for better or worse. Unfortunately I met the man on the train before I met you, and he swept me off my feet. If I had met you before him, no doubt the opposite would have happened." She did not believe for a minute what she was saying, but she felt that, in the interests of sparing his feelings as much as possible, she could be allowed a little fabrication. She was convinced that Peter had saved her from a marriage that promised very little in the way of passion or romance. Having now met Thomas in the flesh, she saw no reason to revise that conviction.

"Maryanne, life as the wife of a soldier will not suit you in the long run, I am willing to wager. Not only the tenuous nature of his job, but the low salary, and his frequent absences, will wear you down until you wish you had made another choice."

"Thomas, there is another factor of which you are unaware. I am with child." She moved her hand over her stomach, which was now showing some signs of distension, but which, unless attention were drawn to it and its size explained, could have been assumed to be the result of good living.

Thomas digested this new information. "That does put a slightly different complexion on things, but does not change my overall position. You could give up the child for adoption. In fact, it makes you an even better prospect, from my point of view, since, as mentioned in my first letter to you, I am in need of an heir, and you have now proved yourself capable." He didn't seem to consider the possibility that he himself might not be capable in that area.

The idea of giving up her baby for adoption appalled Maryanne. How could this man assume that the life inside her was just another factor to be removed from the equation? "I would never give up my baby.

He or she was conceived out of love, not by accident, and will benefit from the best that I am able to give him. Or her."

"But that is the problem, Maryanne. What will you be able to offer him or her? I know what the salaries are in the local barracks are, and once you have the added expense of one or more children, you will have to take a step down even from this." And he waved his hand to take in the house.

Maryanne realized that she was not getting through to him. He was now exasperating her, and she saw that plain talk was required. "Mr. Worthington, I am afraid that you are under the impression that everything can be reduced to a monetary level. I realize that times will be tough, and I am prepared for that. However, my husband and I have love for, and devotion to each other. May I compare that with the letters you wrote to me. There was no mention of love, passion, commitment, or any of the other things that a woman needs. And even when you come here, to try and talk me around, still you make no mention of anything of the heart. It is all an accounting exercise to you. And the fact that I am pregnant, which is the culmination of what a woman wants from life, is merely an inconvenience to you, and is to be discarded at the earliest opportunity. And, if anything, is proof of my fecundity, and my ability to allow you to pass on your profits to an heir. Thomas, you mentioned in your most recent letter that you had no understanding of women. I am afraid that I must tell you that the situation is worse than you imagined. You have no idea at all of how women work, or what they want. You will need to improve immeasurably in that area before any woman shows any interest in you. Sorry to speak bluntly, but I see that simple protestations on my part are not getting through to you."

Thomas sat there, a little stunned at this tirade. He was not sure how to handle it. Finally he said "I do realize that I am largely inexperienced in affairs of the heart. That is due to a secluded upbringing, and devoting my attentions to my business to the exclusion of all else for the last fifteen years or so. I had hoped that, once we were together, you would show me how these things work, and instruct me in the needs and wants of a woman."

At this, Maryanne felt rather abashed at what she had said. Thomas was finally displaying a human, vulnerable side, and showing that it was not all an accounting exercise to him. She decided to ameliorate her tone. "I'm sure you will find a woman who will be all that you require, and who will lead you through the maze that is a woman's needs and desires. I might have been that woman once, but I am no longer, I am sorry to say."

Thomas saw that there was no point in pursuing this, and he took his leave, rather morosely.

Maryanne sat there for a long time after he had gone. For all his lack of appreciation of her feelings, she felt sorry for him, and she found herself wishing that he found someone who would be the woman he needed.

Chapter 3

As the baby grew inside her, she experienced the usual effects that pregnancy does. She got tired more quickly, with the extra weight she was carrying, and had occasional severe bouts of back pain.

Peter was supportive during this time, even if he could not really understand how it was happening.

They found a midwife living nearby, and made arrangements for her to assist them when the time came.

Finally the day arrived when Maryanne knew that the birth was imminent. Luckily Peter was not on duty, and he was dispatched to summon the midwife.

Maryanne had a relatively easy, but certainly not painless labor, and gave birth to a healthy baby boy. Peter assisted where he was able.

Afterwards, Maryanne lay with the baby on her chest, and looked tenderly at him. "Isn't he beautiful?"

"Yes, I suppose so." Peter found it as difficult to dissemble as Maryanne. He could appreciate that the creation of life was a wonderful and mysterious thing, and was something that only women understood. And that the baby now lying on her had potential to become all sorts of things. But he was not able to consider him beautiful. But Maryanne thought he was, so that was sufficient.

"I've been thinking about names, in case it was a boy. What about 'Albert'? It was my uncle's name."

Once again, Peter didn't have strong feelings on the subject. Albert was as good as Frederick was as good as Joseph. "Yes, that is fine by me."

Maryanne and Peter were about to discover another disadvantage of living far away from family. Maryanne had no mother or similar female assistant to help her in the early days with Albert. She had found a couple of books on the subject of child rearing, and had devoured them, but there is no substitute for experience, and she found herself often at a loss as to what to do in certain situations. She didn't know what most mothers work out with their second or successive children: that babies are a lot more resilient than they seem, and there are not many situations or occurrences that are really serious. Maryanne didn't know this, and she worried every time Albert cried or seemed out of sorts. He thrived, however, and she gradually came to understand what interventions were necessary in which situations.

Peter, however, felt a different dynamic in the house. He began to feel more and more that he was the least important member of the household, and that he was no longer first in Maryanne's affections. She looked at Albert with the same loving tenderness that she used to use with Peter. Now, when she looked at Peter it was a neutral look, or even one of exasperation or irritation when he didn't seem to understand Albert's needs or wants, when Peter occasionally held him or rocked or walked with him. Peter was discovering what every new father discovers: that, at the most basic or animal level, his role of helping to produce the offspring was now complete, and his remaining role was simply to provide, while the female performed the raising of the children. He could see that something like this was happening, but he couldn't understand why the addition of another small member of the family should alter everything so completely. He was fighting millennia of evolution.

And so, since Maryanne seemed to have so little time for him, he began to spend more time at the barracks than previously. He found excuses to stay longer on the days he had to go there, and even occasionally found excuses to go there when he wasn't required at all.

The other fathers in the barracks recognized what was going on, but as was the custom in those days, and still is in many ways, they didn't talk about it.

Albert grew steadily, and began to take notice of what was happening around him. As he grew, he seemed to understand that he needed to make an effort to bond with his father, and he would smile and gurgle whenever he saw Peter. This had the effect of slowly bringing Peter around to realizing that Albert was not simply an addition to the family, but was a fully-fledged member and was earning his place. Peter then began to understand Albert better, and respond to his moods and requirements more easily. He spent more time with Albert, and began to find this time more and more rewarding.

One aspect of having children that Maryanne had been warned about, certainly came to pass, and that was the expense of raising children. As it was, Peter's salary had been just enough to keep the two of them. Albert and his occasional unusual needs stretched their budget past breaking, and they had to economize even further. Maryanne reflected that she had been warned about this by more than one person. She, however, felt that it was worth the deprivation. The feeling of being a mother trumped all other considerations.

Chapter 4

One day Albert awoke and didn't seem quite himself. There had been similar days and Maryanne was not particularly concerned. He seemed to improve slightly during the day. The following day, he was definitely not right, and Maryanne became a little worried. On the third day, he was undoubtedly sick, and she took him to see the doctor.

The doctor examined him, and then pronounced that Albert had measles. "There isn't much specific that you can do for him. Keep him quiet and try and feed him. There's every chance that he will recover after about a week."

Both Maryanne and Peter had had measles when they were children, and they had not had complications, so they were not overly worried. On the following day the typical measles rash developed on Albert. When he was not sleeping he seemed to find his unusual-looking skin interesting, and held his arm close to his eyes to inspect it.

Things went like this for a further two days, and then on the following day, Albert showed signs of labored breathing. Maryanne was worried at this, and returned to the doctor.

"Unfortunately, Albert has developed pneumonia, which is a common complication from measles. He needs to be admitted to hospital."

Maryanne replied "We don't have the money to put him in the hospital. Can we not nurse him at home ourselves? My husband is not currently away on duty, so he will be able to help."

"You can, but the nursing staff have more experience in handling this sort of thing. If you really can't afford it, then I'll give you the required medication and you'll have to nurse him yourself."

Maryanne returned with the medication the doctor had prescribed. She told Peter about the situation. "We're going to have to nurse him. And I think we are going to have to watch him continuously. We shall have to take shifts."

She and Peter worked out a routine where each sat next to Albert's crib for a time, while the other slept, or cooked, or relaxed. As much as one can relax when one's child is ill.

Unfortunately, Albert didn't improve. His breathing became more forced. He seemed to be fighting the infection almost physically. He would be restless, and make little violent movements as if he were trying to push the sickness away. Maryanne and Peter watched him, and felt helpless.

During that night Peter was watching him, and noticed that he seemed to be resting better. He seemed to be no longer fighting the infection, and although his breathing was still forced, he seemed to be past the worst. Peter returned to the book he was reading. After about 10 minutes, he looked at Albert, and Albert's chest was not moving at all. Peter jumped up, and picked the child out of his crib. There were no signs of life. "Maryanne, wake up!" he shouted.

Maryanne jumped out of bed. She felt for a pulse. There was none. Albert had gone.

She sank onto the bed and wailed. Peter replaced the lifeless child back in the crib, and sat next to Maryanne. He had no idea what to do. He didn't want to cry, he didn't want to comfort Maryanne. He felt lifeless too. He eventually left the house and walked around the streets, his mind as blank as if he had never had a thought in his life. He moved mechanically, but eventually found himself back at the house. Maryanne was still on the bed, now sobbing quietly. He lay next to her, and put his arm around her. She moved up against him and carried on crying. They lay like that for the rest of the night.

In the morning Peter got up before Maryanne, wrapped Albert's body in a blanket, and took it outside. As soon as the General Store was open, he went and bought some rough wood, and made a rudimentary coffin for Albert. He placed the body in it and nailed it shut. The finality of this act finally broke his defenses, and he sat down and wept.

After a time he went back into the house. Maryanne was awake, but just lying on the bed, looking at the wall.

Later that morning Peter arranged for a funeral, with the same pastor who had married them. While there, Peter spoke to him about Maryanne. "Is there anything I can do to make things easier for her?"

The pastor was sympathetic, but realistic. "You must understand that Maryanne has effectively lost a part of herself. In the same way that Eve was created out of part of Adam, a child is created from part of its mother. She will never get over this completely. The best you can do is to simply be there. She may act oddly, and do things that make no sense to you. Just be sympathetic, and don't try and rush her. She will eventually get nearly back to how she was."

What Peter didn't ask the pastor, was how he was meant to recover from Albert's death himself. As a man he felt that he was meant to keep the ship of his family afloat, without being rocked by the waves. But he had bonded strongly with Albert, after his initial indifference, and he now felt the death keenly. But men were meant to act like men, and so he refrained from mentioning his own state of mind.

Albert's funeral was held three days later. Some of Peter's comrades from his barracks attended, and the landlady that Maryanne had befriended when she first arrived in Omaha. Peter and Maryanne went through with it mechanically, responding to sympathy wishers appropriately, but without even being aware a lot of the time what was happening. Afterwards they returned home, and Maryanne broke down and wept again. Peter wished that he could too, but he felt that he had to be strong. He sat there, feeling helpless.

Chapter 5

The months following Albert's death were quiet, bleak, and grey. Peter and Maryanne hardly spoke to each other, and almost lived separately.

Over the times that Peter was away on duty with the Pacific Railroad, Maryanne sat and looked out the window. She had lost interest in most things, and barely ate enough to keep alive. When Peter was home, they went about their lives, but without enjoyment.

Slowly, however, Maryanne resumed her interest in sewing, and crocheting. She started to make a blanket for them for the upcoming winter months. She started to cook again. While she was certainly not the joyful person she had been, she was definitely on the road to recovery.

Peter however, seemed to be unable to recover. He was moody, and incommunicative, and hardly ever initiated a conversation with Maryanne. He responded to her overtures monosyllabically, and seemed to be unwilling to talk about anything.

One evening Maryanne decided to try and get through to him. She sat next to him. "Peter, dear, you seem to be very morose. Are you still grieving for Albert?"

Peter looked away. He was in a turmoil. Should he break down in front of his wife, and thus display apparent weakness, or should he brazen it out and pretend that he was not unduly affected by Albert's death? Unfortunately he chose the latter path. "It's nothing really. I'm more concerned for you. Are you getting over it?"

If Peter had taken the path he perceived to be the weaker one, the story of Maryanne and Peter's lives would have had a completely different ending. However, for all sorts of reasons - his upbringing, his military training, and others, he decided that he could not confess his innermost feelings to Maryanne, and so the grief carried on festering inside of him.

Maryanne could tell that he was not being fully open with her, but she didn't know how to get him to open up. Their lives carried on as before.

About a month later Peter joined a patrol that went out onto the plains some distance from Omaha, to confront some Indians that were raiding nearby white settlements. He left early in the morning, said a perfunctory goodbye to Maryanne, and was gone. He said that he would most probably be away for about three days.

Maryanne spent that day washing, preserving some fruit, and reading. The next day she was sitting sewing, and around midday, there was a knock at the door. She opened it, and Stephen, one of Peter's comrades, stood there. She took one look at his face, and her legs turned to water.

"Hello, Maryanne, may I come in please?"

"Cer.., certainly." she stammered. She managed to get to a chair herself before slumping into it. She tried not to look at Stephen.

Stephen sat down. "Maryanne, I need to tell you something. I am afraid I am the bearer of bad news." He paused.

Maryanne could feel her throat constricting and her vision blurring. She was close to fainting.

"I am deeply sorry to have to tell you that Peter was shot and killed while we were engaging some Indians, early this morning."

Maryanne caught a sob in her throat. Stephen wondered whether he should comfort her, but felt it would not really be appropriate. He wasn't quite sure what to do. He had never had to perform this kind of duty before.

"I am really sorry. He was a good friend of mine too."

After a minute or two, he felt that there was no point in staying. He stood up. "His funeral will be held at the barracks. I shall come again in the next few days to give you the details." He let himself out.

Maryanne succumbed to a sort of grey semi-consciousness. She wasn't fully awake, but she wasn't asleep either. Her brain slowed down, mercifully sparing her from having to think about anything. She remained in this state of limbo for a couple of hours.

Finally she had to rouse herself. She took to her bed, and fell asleep, and slept the rest of the day, and all night.

The next day she opened her eyes, and remembered everything. She lay there wondering about life. Was there a God, who intentionally gave happiness, in order that he may snatch it away again? Or was it part of some bigger plan, that was meant to prepare one for some future existence? Was there a plan at all? Was there a God at all? She had no answers. All that she knew was that six months ago her life had been idyllic. Now it was shattered.

She dragged herself through that day, and the next one.

On the following day Stephen came to give her details of the funeral, which would be held the following day.

The next day she dressed mechanically, in black. Luckily she had something in black and didn't have to go out and buy a dress. She left the house and walked slowly to the barracks. Stephen met her and guided her to where the funeral was to be held.

She managed to get through the service without breaking down. Afterwards, some of Peter's other brothers-in-arms came and offered their condolences to Maryanne. After most of them had left, she said to Stephen "Did the Indians trap Peter somewhere? How did he actually get shot? I always thought that he was wily enough to avoid getting into a dangerous situation."

"Strange you should ask that! I wasn't sure if I should tell you this or not. But since you asked: the circumstances in which Peter was shot were not typical at all. He was in cover, and would have been perfectly safe if he had stayed there. But for some reason, I'll never know why, he left cover and walked out into an area that was very exposed. And he would have known that. Within seconds he had been spotted by an Indian and they fired. He was down with one bullet. It was almost as if he had wanted to be shot."

Maryanne understood immediately, but didn't say anything to Stephen. If only Peter had opened up to her, and begun the healing over Albert's death. But he decided to do the 'manly' thing and bottle it up. And it festered and grew inside him, until the only way out he could see was to die, as honorably as possible. The news left her desolate. She walked slowly back to the house, hardly noticing the people around her.

Chapter 6

The day after the funeral, Maryanne awoke and lay there pondering on the way her life had changed over the past two years.

From the calm and security of her aunt's house, she had moved to a far more tenuous existence, while being happier than she had ever been. That had now been replaced by grief and loss, while her existence remained tenuous. Where, only just over a year ago, she had wondered whether life could get any better, she now wondered whether life could be any worse. She had lost a child, lost a husband, and had no source of income. The small payout she had received from the army would cover her rent and food for six months at the most, if she lived frugally. But what then? Should she return to stay with her aunt? Or, she tried not to even form the thought in her mind, should she ask Thomas to finally take her as his wife?

She realized that asking Thomas to take her certainly was an option, and one of the better ones available to her. But there were so many reasons that she fought with the idea. Her original reason for rejecting him now seemed relatively trivial. His seeming inability to show love and passion was now hardly worth worrying about. She had had love and passion in abundance, and where had it finally got her? She had loved a child and lost. She had loved a husband and lost. She wondered whether it really would have been better to never have loved at all.

The main reasons she could not countenance throwing herself on Thomas's mercy was the indignity of effectively begging him, now that the roles were reversed, and the real possibility, in fact the better than even chance, that he would refuse or even ignore her request.

However, as the days wore on she slowly came round to the idea. She realized that she would be prostrating herself, but not very much worse than Thomas had prostrated himself to her when he visited her in Omaha. Plus, it was purely between the two of them. It was not as if she was publicizing her request. Whatever his answer, it would be private to them, and she would not have to suffer the judgment or feigned sympathy of other people. Finally, for all his dourness and seeming coldness, he had acted with honor throughout, and she had no reason to imagine that he

would act any differently in this situation.

Finally, she realized that she had nothing to lose. If he refused, she would return to Baltimore.

She sat down and wrote.

>Dear Thomas,

>It is with great difficulty that I write this letter, as I am sure you will understand once you have read it.

>My circumstances are greatly altered since the time you came to see me in Omaha. Since then, I gave birth to a baby boy. At about six months old, however, he became ill, and we could not afford the medical expenses to treat him effectively. He died shortly thereafter. That effectively drove a wedge between my husband and me. Whether it was my own sadness at losing my child, or whether it was his own sadness at the loss, I am not sure, but my husband became withdrawn and incommunicative. Not long after that he was shot and killed while on patrol on the plains. From information gathered from another member of his barracks, it would seem that he could have kept himself out of harm's way, but instead exposed himself to gunfire.

>I am thus, circumstantially anyway, back to how I was as I boarded the train in Baltimore. However, I am vastly different in experience. I have loved and lost, and I am

ready to seek contentment. I do not desire romance any more. However, I should like to have more children.

And so I come to the main purpose of this letter.

I am writing to say to you that, should you still be in need of a wife, and still feel that I may fill the role, I shall be happy to join you in San Francisco. I do not have the requirements that I mentioned when you visited me here, any longer. However I have learned much about housekeeping and child rearing, and thus should be able to fulfill your requirements, as mentioned in your letters, and on your visit.

Kindly reply soonest, since I shall only have enough money for the train fare should I leave within the next two months. Should I not hear from you within that time, I shall return to Baltimore.

Yours etc.

She re-read what she had written. She felt it struck exactly the right tone. It was not contrite, since she had nothing to be contrite about. It was not supplicatory either. It simply stated the facts, and offered to resume their arrangement, albeit two years later.

She posted it, and carried on with her depressing existence.

Chapter 7

Three weeks later, a letter arrived from San Francisco. Maryanne sat down, too a deep breath, and opened it.

> Dear Maryanne,
>
> I am sorry to hear of your recent losses. I cannot imagine what it must be like to lose a child.
>
> I was more than a little surprised to read your offer, since you seemed so adamant that I was not the right man for you when I visited you in Omaha. However, as you point out, circumstances change, and the experiences one has, temper one's needs and wants.
>
> I am still not married. After what you said to me in Omaha I understood that I needed to learn more about the ways of women. However, I could not really see my way clear to doing that easily. I don't mind telling you that I have thought of you often since our meeting in Omaha.
>
> After due consideration, I am willing to accept your offer, and for us to resume our arrangement once you arrive here. Kindly notify me of your arrival date.
>
> Yours etc.

Maryanne sat and read it again. Short and sweet, but all that was necessary, she thought. And he had been thinking of her since his visit! Maybe a heart did beat in that accountant's breast after all!

Maryanne went outside and looked at the sky, or as much as was visible between the buildings. It was a deep blue, and seemed to radiate hope. For the first time in many months she felt that life might improve.

She took a large part of her meager savings, and bought a ticket to San Francisco. However, this time she had to make do with sharing with other women. Needs must. She arranged to terminate the lease on the house, and to sell most of the furniture that she and Peter had bought. She made ready to depart.

She also wrote to her aunt. After informing her of her recent losses, she continued:

> After much agonizing, I decided to contact Mr. Worthington again, to see whether he was still in need of a wife, and if so, whether he was interested in our resuming our previous arrangement. He replied in the affirmative, and I am shortly to be leaving Omaha for San Francisco. I have often thought how similar your earlier life and mine are turning out to be. It is as if my sojourn in Omaha provided the experience of love and passion that I needed to have, and allowed me to have my fill. Now, older and wiser, I shall be content with a good, solid man, and hopefully more children. I don't like to think of Omaha simply as a detour on the bigger road of my life, but that is what it seems to have turned out to be.
>
> I shall write again once settled with Thomas.
>
> Yours, etc.

The day of departure arrived. While getting dressed, she remembered that the dress she was wearing was the same one she had on when Peter led her up on to the roof of a rail car, when it had gone through a tunnel and she had got soot everywhere. She smiled ruefully. That all seemed so long ago now. She had lived almost a lifetime since then.

She got a cart to the station, and had her trunk placed in the baggage car. She climbed aboard and joined two other women in a compartment, larger than the one she had been in on her earlier journey.

As the train slowly pulled out of Omaha station, she felt that she was leaving behind a large chunk of her life. Much good, but much bad too. Much like life in general. But it was a sunny day, and she looked to the west and the start of a new chapter.

As they pulled into San Francisco, she saw Thomas waiting on the platform. He had flowers in his hands again. At least he gets that part right, she thought wryly.

She alighted and went up to him.

"Hello Thomas. I am glad to see you again."

"Hello Maryanne, I am glad that you have finally arrived in San Francisco." He bent and kissed her lightly on the cheek, and then proffered the flowers. She took them and smelt them. They had a fresh, clean fragrance.

"Thank you."

Thomas had brought two servants with him, and he instructed them to get Maryanne's trunk. He led her out of the station to a waiting buggy, and helped her aboard.

They rode through the streets and she took in the city. It was much bigger than Omaha, from what she could tell, and it was a lot busier too. At one point in the ride she looked down on the sea, and she realized that she had not seen the sea for two years. Finally they turned into the driveway of one of the larger houses that she had seen. They stopped at the door, and it was opened by a man who looked like a butler.

"Good afternoon, madam!" he said.

"This is James. This is Miss Marston." said Thomas. Then he looked quickly at Maryanne. "Ah, but you're no longer Miss Marston, are you?" he said quietly.

"No, I am not. But it will suffice for now!" she smiled.

Thomas showed her into a hallway, and she met another woman servant, Mabel, who was the housekeeper. Thomas led her up a large staircase, and at the top they turned right. "The main rooms are on that side, and you will have rooms here, for now." He showed her her quarters, each room of which was about the same size as the entire house she had lived in, in Omaha.

"I have arranged a reception for tomorrow night, for you to meet some of my friends and business associates. I hope that that is all right."

"That is fine. I look forward to meeting them. Will, er, the Thackerays be there?"

"Yes, they have indicated their attendance. I think possibly George will take a while to be won over, but Martha is always understanding. I need to now return to the factory, to attend to some business. Please make yourself at home, and ask James or Mabel should you need anything. Actually, that doesn't need to be said, does it? You don't need to make yourself at home, since this is your home!" He gave Maryanne a quick hug, and then left.

Maryanne sat on the bed and looked about her. The difference from her room in Omaha was marked. Apart from the size, everything about it was obviously good quality. The furniture, the bedding, the carpet, all were of a high standard.

She lay back on the bed and wondered whether she actually deserved all this. And she resolved then to make Thomas a good wife, and to contribute to his life, and life in San Francisco generally, as much as she was able.

Chapter 8

Arrangements for the wedding began almost immediately. Thomas had chosen a local church for the ceremony, but took Maryanne there to check whether she approved of it. She did.

He took her to a dress shop and left her there to be measured for her wedding dress. He then fetched her and they went to discuss food with the caterers. Then, on the way home, they went to visit his mother.

Maryanne had had no experience of mothers-in-law. Peter's parents were both dead by the time she met him. She knew that mothers- and daughters-in-law often did not get on well, and she realized that the circumstances of her marriage to Thomas would not count in her favor, but she resolved to do her utmost to befriend Thomas's mother and bring her round.

They stopped the buggy at a pleasant looking house. Not as big as Thomas's, but undoubtedly well-appointed. Thomas led the way to the door, and knocked. An elderly, well preserved lady, about 70 years old, answered.

"Hello mother!"

"Hello Thomas. Let me unlock the door." She rattled a key in the lock, and opened it.

"Mother, I should like to introduce my fiancé, Maryanne. Maryanne, my mother."

"How do you do, Mrs. Worthington?" said Maryanne, proffering her hand. Mrs. Worthington took it briefly.

"Do come in." She led the way into a small but tastefully furnished parlor. "Let me set the tea things."

While Mrs. Worthington busied herself in the kitchen, Maryanne looked around. She saw a young boy in a picture on the mantelpiece. "Is that you?"

"Yes, that's me, fishing in the Patapsco. I never actually told you, did I, that we came from Baltimore originally. That's one of the reasons that your profile on Brides-by-Mail caught my eye."

"Indeed! And there I was, thinking it was my natural beauty!"

Thomas laughed heartily. "It was that that distinguished you from all the other girls from Baltimore!"

Mrs. Worthington sat down and started pouring the tea. "So tell me, my dear, I believe you've had a checkered journey from Baltimore to San Francisco."

Nothing like getting straight to the point, thought Maryanne. She looked quickly at Thomas. She wasn't sure whether her mother-in-law knew her entire past. Thomas's face was inscrutable. Oh well, she thought, no point in avoiding it, best to talk about it now.

"I have indeed. I don't know of anyone else who took two years to do it!" She related the basic story of her sojourn in Omaha, while playing down the fact that she had been on her way to meet Thomas when it began. Thomas could tell her about that, if necessary.

"So you lost your little boy! That is so tragic. I can empathize, since we lost Thomas's twin brother at a similar age. Also pneumonia from measles, as it happens. They both contracted measles, but only little James got pneumonia. That's one of the reasons that Thomas has had a rather sheltered and protected upbringing. We didn't want to lose him too."

"Do you find that you ever got over it?" enquired Maryanne.

"No, my dear, you never fully get over it. I still dream about James occasionally. One gets on with life, but the memory remains. Luckily Thomas has succeeded enough for two sons, so that makes it a little easier." She patted Thomas's knee, and he smiled, having heard this many times before.

"It was devastating losing little Albert, but it showed me one thing at least. I enjoy being a mother. I found it rewarding and interesting. So I hope to be able to provide Thomas with a few heirs at least, and some grandchildren for you."

"Thank you my dear, that will make me very happy."

From her initial coolness, Mrs. Worthington had thawed towards Maryanne on the strength of their shared tragedy. Maryanne understood that her mother-in-law was on her side, and she was grateful for that.

The reception that Thomas mentioned was held that night. About twenty couples, friends and associates of Thomas's, had been invited.

Maryanne shook hands and smiled at them all. She had checked before with Thomas as to how much she should talk about the past two years. He said that it was not necessary to go into any details, but to just tell them that she had been living in Omaha for the duration.

Obviously, however, one couple knew the whole story. When she greeted George and Martha Thackeray she wasn't sure what she was going to say.

"Hello George. Hello Martha. Wonderful to see you again." She thought that that sounded rather lame.

"Hello," said George rather stiffly.

"Hello Maryanne." said Martha. "So sorry to hear of your recent losses."

"Thank you."

After she had greeted the rest of the gathering, Martha came up to her, and steered her away to one side. "I can see such a change in Thomas already! He has cheered up considerably since the last time we saw him."

"I am glad of that. Tell me, how did he take it when you broke the news to him at the end of your train journey from Baltimore?"

"He looked crestfallen. He was standing there with a bunch of flowers in his hand. He saw us, and we walked towards him. He was still looking up and down the train for you as we reached him. When we told him you weren't there he was nonplussed. He could not understand what it was that could change your mind. I tried to explain, but he doesn't really understand women! Hopefully you will now be able to teach him something!"

"Did he tell you that he came to see me in Omaha?"

"No, really? Did he? No, he never mentioned that."

"Yes, about four months afterwards. I was pregnant. He tried to get me to change my mind, without understanding the reasons for my action. I eventually had to spell it out for him. I felt a bit of a heel. But I think I finally got through to him."

"Yes, he understands business issues immediately, but when it comes to people he has to have things explained more than once!"

"And the rest of the time these past two years? Did he never speak about finding someone else?"

"No, actually. And he mentioned you a few times. I think he hoped that you would still finally change your mind. Obviously he never wished the tragedies on you that did happen. But it seems that his patience has finally been rewarded, not so?"

"I suppose so. And George? He seems not to have forgiven me."

"Oh, don't worry about George. He understands women even less than Thomas! He'll thaw over time."

They returned to join the rest of the party.

Maryanne surveyed the group that would be her friends from now on. There were one or two couples that seemed to be close to her age, and she made a point of engaging them in conversation. She would obviously have a duty, as Thomas's wife, to be friendly to his friends, and be the charming hostess, but by the end of the evening she felt that there were definitely some people there that she could relate to. They were not the kind of people who would have lived in a tiny clapboard house on a side street, as she and Peter did in Omaha. But they were the kind of people that her aunt and her might have known back in Baltimore. She was already feeling at home.

Chapter 9

A month after Maryanne's arrival in San Francisco, the wedding took place.

Maryanne wore a pink wedding dress, in keeping with her status as having been married before, and walked down the aisle alone. She had asked Martha to be her Matron of Honor.

The house was gaily decorated for the reception, and there was food and drink in abundance. There were about a hundred guests, and many of them remarked upon how happy and contented Thomas looked, especially compared with the last couple of years.

The bridal couple left for their honeymoon the following day, taking the train south to Los Angeles. They stayed there for three weeks, going to the theatre, art galleries, and restaurants. Thomas also asked, very apologetically, if Maryanne would mind if he visited a few potential customers for his factory. She even accompanied him on one of these trips.

They returned to San Francisco refreshed.

Maryanne settled into life with Thomas. He would go to his factory every day during the week. She stayed at home and busied herself with sewing, reading, and she also decided to learn to play the piano. She engaged a tutor to teach her weekly, and she spent a lot of time practicing.

In the evenings they would have dinner together, and then read, or she would play the piece she had been practicing, for him.

On weekends they would visit friends, or have friends to visit, attend the occasional concert or play, and go for walks in one of the parks, or along the beach promenade.

Maryanne found herself slowly warming to Thomas. Initially she had looked upon this marriage as one almost of necessity; as being required to save her from penury or having to return to live with her aunt. But as the months wore on, her prior indifference to Thomas became affection, and finally love. She understood that it was not the same love that she had had for Peter in the early days of their marriage. That had been a heady, breathless sort of love. But she now knew that that sort of love never remained for long. It couldn't, by definition, since it relied on novelty, and being with someone that one was still getting to know. Once one knew that person well, and there was nothing novel left to do, the headiness had to come down to a regular, day to day sort of togetherness. With relationships that began that way, there was always a vague feeling of disappointment, in that one was aware of its inexorable reduction in intensity, and one wished that it could somehow remain at the initial level.

However, with the sort of relationship she had with Thomas, it improved with time, and thus one was aware of almost a gratitude, that life could improve, rather than deteriorate.

About six months after the wedding, she awoke one day feeling a bit different. This time she knew what it almost certainly was. She waited a few more days, and when it did not change, she went to check with the doctor. He confirmed her suspicions.

That evening, at dinner, Maryanne decided to tease Thomas. "Thomas, dear, do you think this dining table is big enough?"

"Er, big enough for what, my dear?"

"For the extra person who will be joining us soon!"

Thomas looked a little mystified, and then realization dawned. "Really! Are you with child? That is wonderful!" He got up and went and hugged Maryanne around the shoulders. Later that evening they sat on the couch together and discussed how the baby's room should be decorated, and what the child would be named, depending on its gender.

Maryanne had an uneventful pregnancy, and an uncomplicated birth. She produced a boy, which made Thomas very happy. They called him Julian.

At about six months, he also contracted measles, but this time he was whisked off to hospital at the first sign, and recovered without any lasting ill effects.

With the experience from her first child, Maryanne found raising Julian a lot easier, and with help from the servants, she had a relatively easy time as a mother.

Chapter 10

When Julian was about three, Maryanne decided that the time had come to make a trip back to Baltimore to visit her aunt. She corresponded with her, and arrangements were made. Thomas saw the two of them off at the station, and they settled in to the journey. They had a compartment to themselves. Julian was fascinated by everything connected with the train ride, and Maryanne found vicarious pleasure in his interest. He was full of questions, which she answered as best she could.

On the afternoon of the second day the train stopped in Omaha, and since it was going to be there for about an hour, Maryanne and Julian left the train and walked into the town. Not a lot had changed since she was last there. After looking at a few of the shops, they headed for the cemetery. Maryanne had not intended to make any such pilgrimage, but now that she was here, she wanted to go. She found the two graves - Peter's one, and Albert's tiny one.

"Why is this one so small?" asked Julian.

"Because he was only a baby when he died." she explained. She read the birth and death dates on the headstone to Julian.

"I thought babies could never die!"

If only, thought Maryanne. She hugged Julian close, and was thankful for him.

Back on the train, she decided to make a memory for Julian. She took him to the coupling between their car and the adjacent one. She then put him on the ladder going up to the roof, and they slowly made their way up it together, with her behind Julian to protect him. They carried on until their heads emerged above the roof and the wind tousled their hair. Julian loved it, and Maryanne's hair swirled around his face. Maryanne remembered when she did this with Peter, and how they had gone into a tunnel as well, and emerged with soot everywhere.

The sun was about to set just then, and she and Julian watched as the light turned from bright to orange, to gold. She thought about her time with Peter and Albert, and about Omaha. It was as if, while watching the sun, she was finally setting to rest that time, and was letting it go. It was a very freeing thing.

Just after the sun actually set, she and Julian climbed back down again.

Two days later they arrived in Baltimore, and hired a buggy to take them to her aunt's house. Maryanne knocked at the door.

Aunt Hilda opened it. She had aged quite a lot since Maryanne last saw her. "Hello, Aunt! Good to see you after so long! This is Julian. Julian, say hello to your Great-Aunt Hilda."

"Hello." said Julian shyly. Then he turned to Maryanne. "Why is she great? What has she done?"

"She raised me! That's what!" said Maryanne, laughing.

They went into the parlor and sat down. Julian went to explore the garden at the back of the house.

"So, my dear, you have had a whole life's experience since you left. I am sorry for the tragedy you have gone through, but it would seem to me that everything has finally turned out for the best. Am I right?"

"You are indeed. And it is very much as you said it would be. The love and passion that Peter and I had was overpowering in a way, but it satisfied my hunger for such a relationship. Now, with Thomas, life is much more stable, predictable, and easier. I do not hanker for novelty. It's not as if life is boring. Far from it. There is much to do each day that is new. But the affinity between Thomas and me is constant, well-founded, and reliable. I do love him, in a different way, but just as much, as I loved Peter."

"I am so glad that you have finally arrived at a happy place, my dear."

"The only question that remains for me now, is this: when I have a daughter, how do I explain this to her, to save her from having to go through the same tragedy that I did?"

"You can't, my dear. I tried it with you. It didn't work. You have to allow your children to make their own mistakes!"

Maryanne nodded. She finally understood that to be true.

www.ingramcontent.com/pod-product-compliance
Lightning Source LLC
LaVergne TN
LVHW092100060526
838201LV00047B/1493